My Magical Pony

Secret Whispers

The **My Magical Pony** series:

Other series by Jenny Oldfield:

Definitely Daisy
Totally Tom
The Wilde Family
Horses of Half Moon Ranch
My Little Life
Home Farm Twins

My Magical Pony

Secret Whispers

By Jenny Oldfield

Illustrated by Gillian Martin

A division of Hachette Children's Books

Text copyright © 2007 Jenny Oldfield
Illustrations copyright © 2007 Gillian Martin

First published in Great Britain in 2007
by Hodder Children's Books

A Catalogue record for this book is available from the British Library

ISBN-10: 0 340 93245 7
ISBN-13: 978 0 340 93245 2

Printed and bound in Great Britain by
Bookmarque Ltd, Croydon, Surrey

The paper and board used in this paperback by Hodder Children's Books are
natural recyclable products made from wood grown in sustainable forests. The
manufacturing processes conform to the environmental
regulations of the country of origin.

Hodder Children's Books
a division of Hachette Children's Books
338 Euston Road, London NW1 3BH

Chapter One

Krista sang to herself as she mucked out Comanche's stable.

"This is my friend, Lee Harris," Rob was saying to Jo Weston, the owner of the stable yard. Rob and Lee had driven up to Hartfell on a late December afternoon to take a look around the stables. "Lee's from New Zealand. He's travelling round Europe for six months and staying with me over New Year."

"Pleased to meet you, Lee." Jo shook hands then called for Krista to join them. "Come and say hello. This is Lee. Lee, meet Krista.

My Magical Pony

She does all the hard work around here."

Quickly Krista wiped her hands down the sides of her jeans. "Not really," she grinned, shaking hands with Rob's young, fair-haired friend.

"Yes, really!" Jo insisted with a broad smile. "Hey, Krista, show Lee around while I make coffee!"

"What would you like to see?" Krista asked. She felt shy with new people, but Lee seemed laid-back and not at all scary.

"Show me the horses," he replied, as Rob disappeared with Jo into the tack room.

"We're a riding school and trekking centre so we've got mostly ponies," she explained, taking Lee to the winter paddocks. "But this

Secret Whispers

is Apollo. He's a thoroughbred. Jo does three-day eventing with him. And this is Scottie."

"Cool," Lee murmured, looking the two horses up and down.

My Magical Pony

Apollo pulled a chunk of hay from his net and chewed noisily while Scottie, the ex-racehorse, snorted into the cold air and stamped his feet on the frozen ground.

"Scottie looks like he comes from a pretty good blood-line," Lee noted.

Krista nodded then led him to the next paddock. "Do you know about horses?"

"Some," Lee told her, stopping to admire Misty, Shandy and Drifter. "I like this dark bay."

"Yeah, that's Shandy. She's the friendliest pony around! Jo puts beginner riders on her because she never ever acts up. Hey, Shandy!" Krista reached over the fence to scratch the pony's nose. "Now Drifter's different – he's a bit of a handful, aren't you, boy?"

Secret Whispers

Barging Shandy out of the way, the chestnut pony demanded attention. Lee came up to the fence and stroked him. "I can see you love these guys, Krista."

"Totally!" she agreed. "They're all different, but I love them equally! I come here every day during the school holidays – Jo couldn't get rid of me even if she tried!"

Shandy, Drifter, Misty. Comanche the chunky piebald, Duchess the chestnut mare, with her foal, Frankie. One by one Krista introduced Lee to the ponies of Hartfell.

Then Jo called across the yard to say that coffee was ready.

"OK, let's tear ourselves away," Lee grinned. He led the way to the tack room,

My Magical Pony

firing questions at Krista as they rejoined Jo
and Rob. "How long have you been coming
here? … Where do you live? … Do you own
one of the ponies?"

"Since I was five … I
live at High Point
Farm … No, worse
luck!" Krista
replied. *I like him,*
she thought,
taking her mug of
hot chocolate and
perching on a
bench overlooking
the yard. She
glanced sideways

Secret Whispers

at Lee, who was leaning against the doorpost, chatting quietly with Rob and Jo. *He's nice. And I can tell Jo likes him too. Yeah, he's definitely cool. I hope Rob brings him up to Hartfell again.*

"OK, Krista, where do you keep the hoof picks?" Lee asked.

He'd visited the stables every day that week, sometimes with Rob, sometimes alone. He'd driven up from Whitton in all weathers, along the narrow, icy lanes and through the freezing fog. And as soon as he arrived he would offer a hand to muck out, groom or clean tack.

"Hanging beside the tack room door," Krista replied. "On your left as you go in."

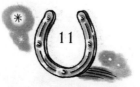

11

My Magical Pony

Lee strolled across the yard, whistling softly. He wore jeans, a black padded jacket and a baseball cap over his fair curls.

"Can you believe him?" Jo muttered as she led Apollo into his stable. "Don't you think he's too good to be true?"

"He's cool," Krista laughed at Jo, who wasn't easily impressed. "Why do you want the hoof pick?" she asked Lee as he came back.

"I need to take it away with me. There's a little Arab pony stabled at a smallholding near Rob's place. I saw she was lame when I drove by her field earlier today, so I thought I'd take a look at her feet."

Krista frowned. "Does her owner know?"

"Her owner – a guy called Ian Charlton,

Secret Whispers

apparently – left her home alone over Christmas and New Year. A neighbour called Jim is looking after her, but Jim doesn't seem to know the first thing about horses. He said it was OK for me to take a look."

"That's good of you," Jo told him.

"Can I come with you?" Krista asked quickly. She'd finished her jobs for the afternoon and was due to meet her dad in town at six o'clock.

"Sure," Lee agreed. "But I've got to warn you that this pony isn't a pretty sight."

"All the more reason!" Krista told him, eager to find out how she might help.

So she and Lee said goodbye to Jo and drove down the lane, chatting as they went.

13

"What did you do in New Zealand?" Krista asked.

"This and that," Lee replied.

"Did you live in the town or the country?"

"My family lives on a farm on North Island."

"So did you work with horses?"

"Now and then."

Krista shrugged then smiled. Getting facts out of Lee was tough work. In any case, he had pulled off the road, down a rough track towards a small stone house with a few shabby outbuildings.

"Is this the place?" Krista asked.

Lee nodded and got out of the car in the gathering dusk. She followed him to the

nearest outbuilding then backed off as the stench hit her. It was a strong smell of soiled straw, as if the creature inside was forced to live in its own filth.

"Remember, I told you it wasn't pretty," Lee muttered. "It looks to me like Jim hasn't mucked this place out in more than a week. And he was leaving the pony out in the field all day until I told him the poor little devil would freeze to death."

"Oh!" Entering the dilapidated stable, Krista gasped. In the gloom she made out a dark shape with matted mane and tail, wearing a tattered, mud-caked rug. "You poor thing!" she cried. She turned to Lee. "What's her name?"

"Jim couldn't tell me that. In fact, he couldn't tell me anything at all, except that Mr Charlton will be back first thing tomorrow."

"She's shivering!" Krista said. "Where's her feed bucket? What does she have to eat?"

"Hay, I guess." Lee inspected the empty

Secret Whispers

net hanging from the wall. "Krista, we're going to stop here a while and sort this little lady out, OK?"

She nodded. As Lee went outside to ring Jo on his mobile phone, Krista cautiously approached the Arab. "There!" she murmured. "Don't be afraid. We won't hurt you."

The chestnut pony cowered in a filthy corner. Her eyes rolled and she laid her ears flat against her head. When Krista drew near, she reared up.

Krista stepped back quickly to avoid the flailing hooves. She heard Lee asking Jo to bring down fresh hay and straw, plus an extra rug that would fit a pony just under fourteen hands high.

My Magical Pony

The pony landed heavily then stumbled sideways. As she struggled to stay upright, Krista saw that she was lame on her back leg. "I don't know how we're going to get near," she told Lee as he came back in.

"OK, we won't try right now," he decided. He made no move towards the pony, only stood in the doorway, waiting for her to calm herself. "She's pretty skinny under that rug," he noted.

"This is so unfair!" Krista cried, looking around at the cobwebs and damp. "How can they keep her in a place like this?"

"Yeah, it's bad," Lee agreed. "But I reckon we can put a few things right when Jo arrives with the stuff."

18

Secret Whispers

"We need to lead her outside so we can muck out." Looking more closely, Krista had spotted a rusty wheelbarrow leaning against the wall. On a shelf above it were dusty brushes and a comb for the pony's mane, plus a frayed head collar and lead rope.

"OK now, sugar!" Lee murmured, slowly edging nearer. He kept his hands at his sides and avoided looking directly into the frightened pony's eyes.

She stood with her legs braced, ready to rear again. But she seemed soothed by Lee's slow approach.

"What happened to you, huh?" he whispered. "Did someone treat you bad? Don't you like to have people come near you?"

19

My Magical Pony

Krista watched as Lee calmed the pony.

He reached out slowly to unbuckle the filthy rug and the movement made her freak out. She reared and tossed the rug to the floor, then charged straight at Lee, who quickly stepped out of the way. "Watch out!" he warned Krista.

She too stepped to one side as the pony bolted into the icy yard, coming to an unsteady halt by the closed gate.

Along the lane, Krista could see Jo's Land Rover bumping down the track. She ran to slow her down and warn her that the pony was loose in the yard.

By the time Jo arrived, Lee had emerged from the stable with the old head collar. Still

Secret Whispers

the little Arab charged frantically around the
yard, in pain and
seemingly
frightened
to death.

"Oh dear!"
Jo took in the
details and
sighed.

The pony's
hooves clattered
on the icy cobbles.
She threw her head
back and reared,
changed direction
and charged again

21

until she was worn out. Then she stopped in the far corner, her sides heaving.

"Oh, look at her!" a shocked Krista cried. The pony was so thin that you could see her ribs. The white star on her forehead was caked in dirt, her thick mane hung over her eyes and she was shivering with fear. "This is awful. What are we going to do?" Krista appealed to Jo and Lee.

Night was falling fast. The pony was cold and starving. If she stayed out in the yard she might freeze to death. Yet who could overcome her fear and get close enough to her to save her life?

Chapter Two

"Lee did it!" Krista told her dad as they drove home to High Point Farm. "He calmed the pony down and managed to get the head collar on."

Krista's dad drove carefully up the winding lane. The car headlights picked out bare thorn bushes at the sides of the road. "Then what happened?"

"Lee borrowed a rug from Jo and got us to muck out the pony's stable while he took a look at her hooves. He found an enormous, sharp stone digging into her back foot.

He dug it out with the hoof pick."

"It definitely sounds like Lee knows what he's doing," her dad remarked.

"Honestly, he was the only one who could get near her. Jo and I both tried, but she just spooked and reared."

Krista's dad nodded as he pulled into the yard at High Point. "So what's Lee's secret?" he asked.

"I haven't a clue!" she replied, rushing into the house to find her mum and tell the story of the poor little Arab pony over again.

"So what happens next?" Krista's mum asked.

She'd got a clear picture from her daughter of a half-starved creature left home alone at

Secret Whispers

the darkest, coldest time of year. And she wanted to know what could be done.

"Jo wants to call the RSPCA," Krista told her. She was in her pyjamas, ready for bed. "But the neighbour, Jim, said we should wait to talk to the owner. He gets back tomorrow."

"OK, that sounds fair enough," her mum decided. Then she kissed Krista goodnight.

I wonder! Krista thought as she lay in the dark. She pictured the Arab pony in her damp, draughty stable. *Even with her new rug, she'll be shivering and lonely. And I bet Ian Charlton doesn't care! If he did, why would he leave her all by herself in the first place, and in that condition?*

Krista turned from one side to the other. Then she tried to sleep on her back. *It's no good!*

she thought, getting out of bed at last and going over to the window. She looked out at the dark, starless sky and called the name of her magical pony – the only one who could help her solve the problem that was keeping her awake.

"Shining Star, it's me, Krista," she began. "I hope you don't think I'm being a nuisance, but I need your advice."

She waited, gazing up at the sky, hoping to see a hazy, silvery cloud appear. This would mean that Star was on his way.

"There's this little Arab pony with a really bad owner," she explained in a low voice. "Lee found her earlier today, and now I'm worried. I can't sleep for thinking about her."

26

From far away Shining Star heard Krista's voice calling him. He spread his wings and flew through the night sky, trailing a cloud of silvery dust.

"What if the RSPCA don't do anything to help?" Krista wondered. "And it's the New Year holiday. It could take them a long time to come."

My Magical Pony

She is troubled, Shining Star thought. *Her voice is filled with fear.*

"The pony could die while we sit here!" Krista murmured. "Shining Star, please come!"

"I am here!" he replied, appearing over the moor in a silvery cloud. His coat sparkled, his broad wings beat softly as he hovered over High Point.

Krista breathed a deep sigh of relief. She felt the warm glow surrounding the magical pony fall on her cold face.

"Tell me more," Shining Star said.

"I think we should take the pony away from where she's living – right now!" Krista told him eagerly.

"And how can we do that?" Star asked

calmly. He held his beautiful head high, letting the wind lift his silken mane from his face, so that Krista could see deep into his dark, wise eyes.

"We can fly there together and set her free before the owner comes back!"

"Set her free to go where? The moors are frozen. The pony could not survive alone in the wild."

Krista frowned. "No, but we could take her up to Hartfell. Jo and I can look after her from now on!"

Shining Star shook his head. "We cannot do that. The owner would be angry."

"So?" Krista cried. "He's been cruel to her. What's it matter if he's angry?"

29

My Magical Pony

"Did you talk to Jo about your idea?" Star asked.

Krista shook her head. "But she won't mind."

Star thought a while. "We must wait," he decided. "Another day will not make the difference between life and death."

Secret Whispers

Krista was disappointed and let it show. "Why can't we fly there now?" she begged.

But her magical pony had made up his mind. "Give Jo time to talk to the pony's owner. If you still need me tomorrow night, call for me."

Looking into Star's eyes, Krista knew that he was right. She nodded slowly.

"And sleep now," he told her. "Remember I will come when you call."

"Eat!" Krista's mum pushed a plate of scrambled eggs and toast towards her. "If you're going to spend all day at the stables as usual, I want you to have a proper breakfast."

My Magical Pony

Krista forced down a few mouthfuls then gulped from a glass of milk. "Can I go now?" she asked.

Her mum nodded. "Your dad's waiting in the car. He'll drop you off on his way to the supermarket."

Quickly Krista grabbed her jacket and dashed outside. "Thanks, Dad. I want to get there early." She willed him to drive fast down the frosty lane.

"Did you talk to Jo on the phone yet?" he asked.

"Yep. I asked if we could rescue the Arab pony and bring her up to Hartfell. She said she'd already been thinking about it, but she wasn't sure." Krista had been up before

dawn, begging and pleading with Jo.

"What does she have against it?" Krista's dad asked.

"She's not sure if there's room, especially if the Arab is half wild. She says, even if Ian Charlton agrees to sell, what good is a pony who can't be ridden?"

"She has a point," her dad admitted. "But are you still hoping to change her mind?"

Krista nodded. For the rest of the journey she planned how they would go down to town with Jo's trailer and buy the pony then drive her back up to a beautiful clean stable at Hartfell. "She'll need feeding up. She's so skinny you can see her ribs!" she told her dad as he dropped her off in the stable yard.

33

"And I'll brush her and groom her until her coat's shining!" she promised.

"Lots of TLC from you, eh?" he grinned and wished her luck.

Dizzy with her plan, Krista dashed off to find Jo, who was leading ponies out to their paddocks. "Well?" she asked, launching straight in. "When can we rescue the pony?"

Jo shrugged. "Whoa, Krista! Like I said on the phone, it's not a case of 'when'. It's a question of 'if'."

"But we have to!" Krista cried. "We can't leave her where she is!"

"I'm not a charity," Jo pointed out. "I can't take in every un-schooled pony who needs a home. We'd burst at the seams within a week!"

Secret Whispers

Krista bit her lip. "Don't you want to help her?" she asked.

Fastening the paddock gate, Jo walked back to the yard. "Of course I do. But I'm trying to harden my heart to say no right now. You see, I don't think we could ever use her on treks. From what I saw yesterday, she'd never be reliable enough."

Hanging her head, Krista wondered why grown-ups had to be so sensible. She felt her hopes sink to rock bottom as Jo talked herself out of rescuing the pony.

"Yeah, I know, you don't have to say anything," Jo sighed, looking hard at Krista's dejected face. "It's not a question of being reasonable, is it?"

My Magical Pony

Krista shook her head. "I just feel so sorry for her!"

"Me too," Jo agreed. She nodded once then pulled out her mobile phone. "I got Mr Charlton's number from Jim yesterday," she explained. "How about I just give him a quick call?"

Krista went from zero hope to sky high in a nano-second. This was cool! Jo was talking to the pony's owner, saying she would like to buy her if he was willing to sell!

Secret Whispers

"… Oh, I see," Jo muttered, her forehead creasing into a frown.

So? Krista wondered. *What's his answer?*

"OK, I understand. Yes, Mr Charlton, I know you've been away over Christmas. But the point is – would you like to sell your pony to Hartfell? … No, I didn't realise … Yes, I get that."

Well? Can we or can't we? Krista couldn't keep still as Jo's conversation came to an end. "What did he say?" she demanded.

"He said no," Jo told her, closing her eyes briefly then taking a deep breath. "Ian Charlton says he's already sold the pony to someone else. End of story."

Chapter Three

Krista went about her morning work at the stable in stunned silence.

"I don't know whether to be glad or not," Jo muttered, brushing Drifter in the next stable.

Krista worked on Comanche, spraying conditioner on his thick mane. "I'm definitely not glad," she confided. "I wanted the pony to come here."

"But at least she's being moved from Ian Charlton's place," Jo pointed out. Drifter's light-brown winter coat was soon brushed to perfection. "That can only be a good thing."

Secret Whispers

"But where to?" Krista wanted to know.

Jo shrugged. "I don't know. Mr Charlton wouldn't say. As a matter of fact, he was pretty rude to me on the phone."

"He probably sold the pony the minute he heard she'd had visitors while he was away."

"I wouldn't be surprised. I know for sure he wouldn't look forward to a visit from the RSPCA." Finishing with Drifter, Jo led him out to his paddock. "Tack Comanche up when you're done," she told Krista when she came back. "I'll be in the house making a few phone calls. Tell everyone we'll be ready to set off at nine-thirty."

So Krista worked on, only looking up to say hi to her friends, Janey and Alice,

39

when they showed up for their morning trek.
"See how smooth and silky your mane is
now," she murmured to Comanche, standing
back to admire the sturdy piebald. "You're all
ready to go. I wonder who's going to be the
lucky person who gets to ride you today!"

Cheeky Comanche poked his nose in her
jacket pocket to fish out any treats that might
be hidden.

"Stop that!" Krista laughed, putting on
his saddle.

The yard grew busy with cars dropping off
more riders. Krista concentrated on getting
ponies ready for the nine-thirty deadline. She
only just made it, leaning against the tack
room door and sighing as the six riders set off.

Secret Whispers

"Good work," Jo told her.

The group disappeared along the cliff path and Jo and Krista were ready to take a break when Rob's red Land Rover arrived in the lane.

"Uh-oh! Rob always knows when I'm about to make coffee!" Jo laughed. "I think he can smell it from his house!"

"Why is he pulling a trailer?" Krista wanted to know. She walked to the gate for a better view. "Jo, come and look!"

Slowly Rob came up the hill. Krista made out Lee sitting in the passenger seat. The trailer trundled heavily behind. "What have they got in there?" Jo frowned suspiciously.

Rob leaned out of his window. "Are you ready for this?" he yelled.

My Magical Pony

From the other side of the car, Lee told Jo and Krista to stand back.

As she did as he told her, Krista heard a shrill whinny from inside the trailer, then the thud of hooves against the metal sides. There was a horse in there, and it wasn't happy! Krista held her breath as Rob slowly turned into the yard.

"OK, I mean it – are you ready for a big surprise?" he said again, parking and stepping out of the Land Rover. "You'll never guess what Lee has just done!"

"Oh, I think we will!" Jo muttered, quickly putting two and two together. She strode round the back of the trailer to peer inside.

"… You didn't!" Krista gasped, staring at Lee

Secret Whispers

as he invited her to step up and take a look.

Lee nodded. "I did."

"I don't believe you!" Krista insisted, peering over the back door of the trailer. "Wow, you did!" she cried.

My Magical Pony

Inside, cowering in a far corner, tethered on a short rope, her eyes rolling in fear, was Ian Charlton's mistreated Arab pony.

"Lee only went and bought her!" Rob explained with a grin. "He drives over there at the crack of dawn and puts in an offer that Charlton can't refuse."

"Oh wow!" Krista breathed, gazing at the terrified creature. "Oh Lee, you rescued her! That is so totally amazing! Oh, I can't even speak!"

"OK, let me get this straight," Jo began.

She, Krista, Lee and Rob were in the tack room. The Arab pony was still in the trailer in the yard.

Secret Whispers

"You want to keep the pony here and pay for her board?"

Lee nodded. "If that's cool with you. By the way, I gave her a name."

"What is it?" Krista asked. She was wreathed in smiles, still hardly able to believe what had happened.

"I'm going to call her Sugar," Lee replied. "'Cos she's the colour of rich brown sugar, except for that white flash on her nose."

"She's going to be really pretty when we clean her up," Krista gabbled. "Arabs have such sweet faces and such big eyes."

"*If* you can get near her with a brush!" Jo pointed out. "I'm not sure we can even get her out of the trailer in one piece."

My Magical Pony

"You just watch Lee," Rob said, following his friend outside and helping him to unbolt the ramp at the back of his trailer.

Lee lowered the ramp gently then stood quite still.

Inside, Sugar whinnied and kicked.

Jo shook her head. "That poor pony is totally traumatised."

"Lee got her in there, and you can bet your bottom dollar he'll get her out again," Rob promised.

And yet, as far as Krista could make out, Lee did nothing except watch and wait.

Gradually however, Sugar calmed down. She stopped kicking and stood quietly, her eyes fixed on Lee.

Secret Whispers

"Watch closely," Rob murmured.

Very slowly Lee put one foot on the ramp and then the other.

Sugar tossed her head but didn't object.

Lee moved forward, hands at his sides, head down. "There, Sugar," he soothed. "I'm not one of those mean types. I won't do you any harm."

My Magical Pony

The pony quivered but held steady. She let Lee move in close.

"Good girl," he breathed, reaching out to untie her rope with a smooth movement then leading her towards the ramp.

The pony followed shakily, snorting occasionally and flicking her ears in every direction.

"I tell you, he's magic with these uptight ones," Rob told Jo and Krista. "I don't know what he does, except I guess he has a direct line to understanding how their brains are wired!"

"He's very good," Jo agreed.

They were all concentrating so hard on Lee's work with Sugar that no one noticed

Secret Whispers

Nathan Steele's mum driving up the lane. She turned into the yard and let Nathan jump out. He shut the car door with a slam.

And that was it. *Bang!* Sugar acted like a gun had gone off. She was halfway down the ramp when she reared up and pulled the rope clean out of Lee's hands. She squealed and landed with a crash, so scared by now that she fell sideways off the ramp, staggered back on her haunches then pulled herself upright.

"Stand clear!" Lee shouted as Sugar charged past Nathan.

The pony cantered right up against the wall that bordered the lane, swung round and with a shrill neigh clattered back the way she'd come.

49

My Magical Pony

There was chaos as Nathan's worried mother yelled instructions and Sugar reared again. This time her hooves struck a stable door, which swung open and banged against the wall.

"That pony's wild!" Nathan's mum cried, dragging her son back to the car.

Jo held Krista and Rob back against the trailer. "No heroics!" she warned. "Leave it to Lee."

But as Krista watched the terrified pony and feared with every passing second that poor Sugar might crash down and injure herself, she wondered if even Lee Harris could bring the wild creature back under control.

Chapter Four

"OK, so now we empty the yard," Lee instructed. He stayed calm, even though Sugar was scared out of her wits.

Following his lead, Jo quietly asked Mrs Steele and Nathan to back into the lane, while Krista and Rob retreated into the tack room.

Lee stood alone, watching Sugar rear then kick out, then race blindly across the yard once more.

"OK, little girl, we know how you feel," he said, his voice barely louder than a whisper. "But nothing bad is going to happen, I promise."

My Magical Pony

Gradually Sugar flicked one ear in his direction. She kept her distance but began to listen to his gentle voice.

"That's good," he murmured. "Now I'm going to stand here until you quieten down, OK? See, I'm not about to hurt you."

The pony seemed to believe him. She slowed down and eventually came to a halt by the tack room.

Secret Whispers

From inside, Krista saw that Sugar was
trembling from head to foot. Her sides
and neck were sweating and she sucked air
noisily through her flared nostrils. *OK, now
Lee can move in and put a rope around her neck,*
Krista thought.

But the young New Zealander looked like he
had no intention of moving closer. Instead, he
stood quite still, looking calmly at the pony.

"What's he doing?" Krista whispered to Rob.

"He's waiting for signals from her."

"What kind of signals?"

"Small stuff. Things that you and I wouldn't
notice."

"Sshh!" Jo warned, fascinated by what was
going on in the yard.

53

My Magical Pony

For a long time Sugar watched Lee and Lee waited. The pony would turn her head slightly towards him, her ears would flick and she would shift restlessly on the spot. Meanwhile, Lee observed her without moving a muscle.

"How patient is that!" Krista breathed.

"Look, she's lowering her head – that's good!" Rob said.

"Why? Why is it good?" Krista wanted to know.

"Sshh!" Jo warned again.

As Sugar's head went down, Lee made his first move towards her. He ducked his own head and took a small step. The pony looked up, her ears flicked nervously. Lee stopped and watched.

54

Secret Whispers

"Maybe I should take him some food to tempt her." Krista thought of a method that usually worked for her.

"No, don't move," Jo said.

"Hey, little girl!" Lee whispered, taking another small step forward. Then another and another.

Krista held her breath, fearing that any moment Sugar would panic and set off again in a mad canter around the yard.

With wide eyes Sugar watched. She let Lee draw near.

"You and me are going to be friends," he whispered, keeping his head down and his arms close to his sides. "Come on, Sugar, come and take a look!"

My Magical Pony

The pony stretched her neck towards the stranger who approached. She took her first step towards him.

"Good girl! How do I seem to you? Am I OK?"

Krista watched as Sugar took another trusting step. She looked swamped by her new rug, her mane was still knotted, her face caked with dirt. But she was calm now and

reaching out for Lee, who let her sniff at his jacket and boots, waiting for her to raise her head again.

"Pretty clever!" Jo murmured.

At last Lee raised his hand to stroke the pony's neck. As he lowered it again, he half turned away, as if he would walk off. He smiled when Sugar took a step to follow him. "Do you want to come with me?" he murmured.

This time he did walk a couple of steps and Sugar followed.

"Ah, so now you want to stay close!" Lee grinned.

Sugar didn't flinch. When Lee walked, she followed.

My Magical Pony

"Wow!" Krista gasped. She saw that Lee was heading towards an empty stable. "He's doing it without a lead rope!"

"It's all about learning to trust," Rob explained. "That little pony probably never trusted anyone in her life before!"

"Hey, Sugar!" Lee whispered, leading her into the stable and quietly closing the door. "You see, things aren't so bad here at Hartfell. This is your new place. Settle down, make yourself at home!"

"I don't know exactly how Lee did it!" Krista told Shining Star.

She was standing at the magic spot in the dying light. Her magical pony had flown all

Secret Whispers

the way from his home in Galishe to see her.

"He kind of whispered and Sugar seemed to understand. She'd gone really crazy because of the car door banging, and you'd have thought that nothing would calm her down again!"

"Perhaps he has a secret that he will share with you," Star said quietly. He was glad to see Krista happy.

She nodded. "Lee says he'll teach me his technique. It's all about learning to pick up signals. It's like a secret language that horses speak that we humans don't usually notice."

Shining Star folded his wings against his sides and rested. He stood in the midst of a sparkling cloud. Glitter dropped on to the dark moor.

My Magical Pony

"What Lee does might look like magic, but it's not really!" Krista went on. "Not your sort of magic anyway!"

Star nodded.

"I mean, Lee can't fly, for a start! He says that all he does is listen and look. He doesn't force it – he waits until the horse is ready to come to him."

"He sounds like a wise man,

Secret Whispers

Krista. You will learn many things from him."

"I know, I can't wait! And I wanted you to know that things have worked out for Sugar. We didn't need to call in the RSPCA or anything. How cool is that?"

The magical pony nodded again then spread his wings. "All is well," he said.

"Because of Lee!" Krista agreed.

"A new year and a new beginning." Slowly Shining Star rose into the evening sky. "I am happy for you, Krista."

"And I'm glad for Sugar!" she smiled.

All really was well as Star beat his white wings and soared away.

Chapter Five

"You have to see it from Sugar's point of view,"
Lee told Krista. He'd picked her up from
High Point and was driving her to Hartfell so
they could begin work with Sugar. "Right
now, on a scale of one to ten she probably
rates human beings at below zero."

"Yeah, I don't blame her." As they rattled
up the lane and the stables came into view,
Krista remembered the filthy stable at Ian
Charlton's smallholding. "That was a rotten
way to treat a pony!"

"For all we know, most of her memories are

Secret Whispers

bad," Lee went on. "Every time anyone comes near her, she's mistreated – for a start, taken away from her mother before she's ready, she's dragged from place to place, cooped up in the dark, half-starved …"

"Don't!" Krista shuddered. No wonder the pony was almost wild.

"Our job is to show her we're not all like Ian Charlton."

Krista frowned, looking out on moors that were covered in heavy frost and up at dark grey clouds. "What was he like?" she asked.

Lee shrugged. "Ian Charlton? Small guy, long dark hair, nothing special."

Krista knew that this was all she would get out of Lee on the subject. And anyway,

they were pulling into the yard at Hartfell. Jo was carrying tack from the tack room and the day was about to kick into action.

Four riders had set off on the morning trek; Jo had called for John Carter, the vet, to look at a saddle sore that had developed on Kiki's back; and still Krista and Lee stood quietly at the door of Sugar's stable.

"When do we go in and work with her?" Krista wanted to know.

"When she's ready," Lee replied. He leaned on the stable door, totally relaxed. "She's been thinking about it, wondering if we're OK."

"How can we tell when she's decided?" The first thing Krista had learned this morning

64

was the "P" word – Patience. If you wanted to work with a problem pony, you needed loads of it. "Are you waiting for her to lower her head, or what?"

"When she's ready, she'll come to us," Lee explained, keeping his voice low and soft. "She's definitely interested. Look, she's taking her first step."

Sure enough, the Arab pony cautiously approached the door. She sniffed at the sleeve of Lee's jacket and recognised his smell from the day before.

"Can we come in?" he murmured. "Krista here wants to brush that dirt away and make you look pretty." As he talked, he slid back the bolt and gently opened the door.

65

My Magical Pony

Krista followed Lee into Sugar's stable, which was clean and fresh. There was hay in the hay net and water in a yellow bucket in one corner.

"OK, so first we take off this rug. Yeah, good. Now we can have a look at you." Lee moved slowly, without any sudden jerks.

"She's so skinny!" Krista gasped. Sugar's hipbones made sharp angles. Every rib stood out along her sides. But she was a gorgeous rich brown, with a lighter mane and tail. Her legs were long and slender, her face beautiful.

"We can soon fix that," Lee promised, glancing up as Jo brought them hot drinks. "I'd say she's probably no more than three years old," he reported. "A whole lot of bad

66

stuff has gone on in her life so far, but Krista
and me, we're planning to put that right."

"I believe you," Jo said with a smile.

As they talked, Krista reached out to
stroke Sugar's neck. The pony flicked her ears
but didn't move away. She looked intently at
the brush in Krista's hand.

My Magical Pony

"Don't you know what this is?" Krista murmured, careful not to scare Sugar with any sudden movement, realising what a big step forward it was for the pony to let them come close. "I'm going to use this to get rid of all those tangles and patches of mud. It'll make you feel a whole lot better."

"Where did you learn how to handle horses?" Jo was asking Lee as they drank their coffee. "Was it back home in New Zealand?"

"I spent some time in California," he told her. "I knew a guy on a ranch there who taught me a few things."

Krista smiled to herself. Lee was so laid back! She was sure that Jo would have her work cut out to discover more.

68

Secret Whispers

"So what's the secret?" Jo asked.

"I look. I listen to what the horse tells me."

Slowly Krista raised the brush and brought it softly across Sugar's withers and along her side. The pony's skin quivered, but she didn't move.

"This is good!" Krista whispered. "This is really cool. Soon you're going to look totally beautiful and perfect!"

"Day two!" Lee announced.

He'd led Sugar into Jo's small arena with its all-weather surface of loose wood chippings. Krista stood at his side, eager to learn more.

"We stand in the middle," he instructed, "and we let Sugar do her own thing."

My Magical Pony

Which meant waiting in the icy wind
that blew down from the top of the moor,
watching the Arab pony wear herself out with
a session of frantic bucking and kicking. Then
she galloped around the edge of the arena, her
mane and tail flying, ignoring Lee and Krista,
who stood and shivered.

"When will she stop?" Krista muttered.

"When she's ready," was Lee's reply. "It's the
usual signal – her head will drop to the ground,
meaning she's not going to pick a fight."

"How did you learn that?"

"I watched wild horses in a big herd in the
Californian desert. Any time a horse wants to
show he's submissive, he lets his head drop
low. And if you want to see when a wild horse

Secret Whispers

is angry, you watch his ears — they flatten right against his head, and he bares his teeth."

"Wow!" This was the longest speech Lee had ever made. Krista was impressed. "I wish we were in California right now!"

"Yeah, it's cold here!" Lee grinned. "But no worries, we're almost ready to do some work."

Watching Sugar closely, Krista saw her slowly lower her head and steady down

to a trot. She had one ear fixed on Lee.

"See, she wants to come to us, but she's still not sure," Lee told Krista. "OK, she's slowed to a walk. And now she's come to a halt."

"So do we walk up to her?"

Lee shook his head. "Not this time. Right now we have to send her away again." Using a long rope which he had slung over his shoulder, he snaked it across the ground towards the pony.

Surprised, Sugar broke into a trot, keeping to the edge of the arena, as far away from Lee's rope as possible. Her head was up again. She was in full flight.

"Why did you do that?" Krista cried.

Secret Whispers

Surely they wanted the pony to trust them and come close.

"So she learns who's boss," Lee explained, flicking the rope and driving Sugar forward. "Every herd has a dominant horse, and for Sugar we have to be that strong guy who'll tell her what to do."

"OK." Krista thought she understood. "You make her run until she's tired, then let her stop."

"You got it. We do that a few times. In the end, her head goes down and we let her walk up to us. She says, 'Thank you for letting me in'. After that, we're alpha male of her herd!"

"She trusts us to be her boss?"

"Right. Watch how it happens. I've never known it to fail."

Chapter Six

"The amazing thing is, it works!" Krista
told her mum.

Lee had been working with Sugar for
four days now, and the pony had made
massive progress.

"She totally trusts Lee and she follows
him wherever he goes. She lets me groom her
and slide her rug on and off. Tomorrow Lee
says we'll try and introduce her to a saddle
and bridle!"

"Wait a minute, is this the same little half-
wild Arab you told me about on Saturday?"

Secret Whispers

Krista's mum asked. Mother and daughter were curled up by the fire, toasting marshmallows which Krista plopped into her mug of hot chocolate.

"Yeah, Mum, that's the point! It's only been four days and you wouldn't believe she was the same pony. She's put on weight and her coat is beginning to shine. And guess what – she even let Comanche and Shandy come up to her in one of the winter paddocks!"

"She's making friends with the others?"

Krista nodded happily. "All because of Lee. He's amazing. I think he could get any problem horse in the world to trust him."

Her mum smiled. "So what's his secret?"

Thinking back over the last few days,

Krista tried to sum up Lee's work with Sugar. "Listening and looking," she replied. "I know it sounds weird, but the way Lee moves and whispers, he kind of speaks horse language!"

"I'm impressed," her mum murmured. "It seems to me that if we knew exactly what he was doing and could bottle it, we'd make an absolute fortune!"

Secret Whispers

*

Thursday morning dawned bright blue and clear – a perfect January day. As soon as she was up and dressed, Krista set off along the cliff path, ready for a morning session when she and Lee would put a saddle on Sugar's back for the first time.

Hi, Shining Star! she thought happily as she passed the magic spot. *We're doing great with the Arab pony. She's made friends with Comanche and Shandy and at this rate we'll have her ready to join the trekking parties by spring!*

The magical pony was flying through the blue sky on a mission in another part of the world when he felt Krista pass by her magic spot. He read her happy thoughts.

"Krista is content," he said to himself, spreading his wings wider and sailing over some snow-capped mountains, across a wide blue sea.

The yard at Hartfell was empty when Krista arrived, so she went to the house, looking for Jo.

"I picked up a message on the answer-phone from Lee," Jo told her. "He's not able to make it today."

"Oh!" Krista's soaring mood suddenly plummeted.

"Yeah, I know, I was surprised too." Putting on her baseball cap and boots, Jo told Krista to listen to the message.

"Hi Jo – Lee here. Something came up. I won't make it

Secret Whispers

today. Tell Krista to carry on without me. See you, bye!"

As Krista listened to the message, her stomach churned. *Tell Krista to carry on without me.* "Help!" she muttered. "How am I supposed to know what to do?"

By now Jo was ready for work and she held the door open for Krista. "Typical Lee, not to say what came up. Getting information out of him is like getting blood from a stone."

Krista led the way on to the yard. "But it must be important. He wouldn't just ditch Sugar after all he's done."

Jo sighed. "Let's hope!" she murmured, taking hold of a wheelbarrow and heading for the nearest stable.

*

My Magical Pony

Do what you've seen Lee doing for the last four days, Krista told herself.

She was in Sugar's stable, standing in a corner, quietly watching and listening. *Stay totally calm. If you get wound up, Sugar's going to pick it up and start acting twitchy.* "That's it, good girl!" she whispered as the pony approached.

Sugar came and took a good sniff at Krista's jacket. She reached her head over the stable door and peered across the yard, as if looking for Lee.

"This is a big thing for me," Krista murmured in Sugar's ear. "It's the first time Lee's left me on my own. I'm hoping I don't mess up!"

80

Secret Whispers

The pony lowered her head and gave Krista a friendly nudge.

"Hey, girl! Today I have to put a saddle on you," Krista explained. "Now a saddle is just a piece of leather – it's nothing to be scared of. Look, Shandy wears one all the time."

My Magical Pony

Out in the yard, Jo was preparing Shandy for the morning trek. She tightened the girth strap and lowered the stirrups for Nathan to mount.

"A saddle makes things more comfortable for you when someone rides you," Krista went on. She saw that Sugar's ears were pricked and that she was paying attention to the ponies in the yard. "OK, I know this is a steep learning curve for you. It is for me too!"

Come back, Lee! she thought. *This is too much for me to do by myself!*

"OK, Krista?" Jo asked as she passed hurriedly by.

"Yes, good thanks!" Krista sounded more confident than she felt. She stayed in the

Secret Whispers

stable with Sugar, waiting until the trek had set off and the yard was empty.

Sugar sniffed again at Krista, investigating first her jacket and then her boots. She seemed relaxed, so Krista gently unfastened her rug and put on a head collar. But then a sudden movement startled the pony and she pulled back.

"Sorry!" Krista whispered, remembering the all-important "P" word. "That was me being in too much of a hurry. But it's OK, we needn't rush. We can stay in here as long as you like."

Gradually Sugar settled again and she relaxed on the end of the rope. Her breathing was even, her ears were pricked.

My Magical Pony

"Ready?" Krista asked, leading the pony out of the stable at last. "We're going for a little walk."

Out they went into the cold yard where the sun cast long shadows. Krista walked Sugar full circle, through sun and shade, until they came again to her stable.

"You're so good!" Krista breathed, leaning her head against the pony's cheek. She felt thrilled at what they'd done so far. Now all she had to do was to fetch the saddle from the tack room and put it on!

"Nice work!" Jo told Krista when she got back from the ride.

Krista and Sugar were still working

Secret Whispers

together. Sugar was on a lunge line, there was a saddle on her back and she was cantering smoothly around the arena.

"We did it!" Krista grinned. She loved how the little Arab moved – smoothly and proudly, with her supple neck arched and her head held high.

"I'm amazed." Jo came and leaned on the fence, studying every move. "Whatever Lee does – these secret whispers, or whatever – he's definitely passed the method on to you!"

Krista was thrilled. Sugar trusted her, and it was the best feeling in the world!

My Magical Pony

The pony cantered on, one ear fixed on Krista, the other focused ahead. Then Krista shortened the lunge rein and she slowed to a trot, finally approaching Krista in the centre of the arena. "Isn't she beautiful?" Krista murmured.

"A little sweetheart," Jo agreed. "But I'm still wondering where Lee's got to."

"Call Rob and find out," Krista suggested. She stroked Sugar's soft nose then rubbed at the white star between her eyes, sending Sugar into pony heaven.

"Good idea," Jo decided, striding off towards the house.

It was pamper time. Sugar had worked hard in the arena that morning and now Krista was

Secret Whispers

brushing her down from head to toe until her chestnut coat shone.

"How does it feel to be a grown-up girl and have a saddle on?" Krista asked, brushing gently on the underside of Sugar's long neck. "You looked like Shandy and the others out there in the arena!"

Sugar took a deep breath then sighed contentedly. Her long, copper-coloured mane was silky-smooth, falling prettily over her eyes and down one side of her neck. It was only when a car with a trailer rattled noisily up the lane that her muscles stiffened and a touch of fear appeared in her dark eyes.

"Who's that?" Krista wondered out loud, watching warily as a woman driver turned

into the yard then got out of the car and slammed the door.

The noise sent Sugar skittering across the stable. She hid in the darkest corner.

The woman stood hands on hips and took a good look around. She was tall and skinny, dressed in a dark-blue padded waistcoat, cream jodhpurs and black boots.

When she spotted Krista at the door of the stable, she strode across.

"Who's in charge around here?" she asked in a loud voice.

88

Secret Whispers

"Jo's in the house," Krista told her, going out to meet her. "Jo Weston. She owns Hartfell." Sugar kept to the corner of her stable, beginning to tremble and kick out, like in the bad old days.

"Jo Weston? That's not what I was expecting to hear. Does the name Lee Harris mean anything to you?" the stranger demanded. She tried to look over Krista's shoulder to see who was kicking up the fuss in the stable behind her.

"Lee's not here," Krista replied. She didn't like the woman's loud voice and nosey manner.

"Who have you got there?" the visitor asked, pushing past Krista and peering into Sugar's stable. "Yep, just as I thought!"

"What's wrong? What are you doing? Hey!"

89

My Magical Pony

To Krista's surprise, the newcomer had begun to slide back the bolt on the door.

"Stand back, this pony's vicious," the woman warned, unhitching Sugar's head collar from its hook by the door. "You can't reason with her. You just have to wade in and be tough."

"How do you know? Listen, that's Lee's pony. You shouldn't be doing that!"

Running into the stable after her, Krista grabbed the woman's arm and tried to drag her out again. Meanwhile, Sugar had reared up and brought her front hooves down dangerously close to Krista's straining figure.

"What on earth ...?" Jo's voice interrupted

Secret Whispers

the struggle. She'd come out of the house to inspect the car and trailer, then run across to the stable when she'd heard the scuffle. "Krista, get out quickly. And if you've got any sense, you'll do the same," she told the stranger.

The woman grunted and backed out of the stable. "I was looking for Lee Harris," she told Jo. "But apparently he's scarpered and left you to deal with the problem!"

"What problem? Who are you?" Jo asked firmly, squaring up for an argument.

"The problem I'm talking about is that vicious little Arab in the stable back there," the woman answered.

"She's not vicious!" Krista cried. "Her last

91

owner, Ian Charlton, didn't look after her properly. That's why no one could get near her."

Secret Whispers

"Hush, Krista," Jo warned then turned back to the stranger. "Lee bought the pony from Mr Charlton. So what's she got to do with you?"

"I'm Julie Charlton," came the angry answer. "Ian's ex-wife."

Krista bit her lip. Jo allowed a deep frown to crease her brow. Neither said a word as the visitor ranted on.

"You've all been taken in – the pony wasn't Ian's to sell!" Mrs Charlton claimed, dipping into her jacket pocket and drawing out a long white envelope. "I'm the one who owns that little Arab, and I have the papers to prove it!"

Chapter Seven

Julie Charlton told Krista and Jo that Sugar's real name was Diamond Charm.

"That's because of the white diamond on her forehead," she explained. "I bought her as a yearling, two years ago. I already owned two grey Arabs. Since then, my beloved ex-husband's business collapsed, we lost our eighteenth-century manor house and we ended up in that terrible, run-down place by the coast road."

"What happened to the two greys?" Jo asked. She'd invited Julie Charlton into the

house so they could talk things through.
Reluctantly, Krista had followed.

"Oh, I already off-loaded them on to
a friend of mine with pots of money." Mrs
Charlton carelessly waved the question aside.
"She wouldn't take the chestnut though. She
said Diamond Charm was beyond hope – way
too vicious for anyone to handle."

"She's not …!" Krista began.

"Hush!" Jo warned. "When did you and
Mr Charlton get divorced?"

"The final papers came through just before
Christmas. The courts split all the remaining
property between us, and I got to keep
saddles, tack – anything to do with the horses."
Julie Charlton gave off an air of impatience.

"Listen, it's clear Ian was in no position to sell my property, so what I intend to do is reclaim Diamond Charm – quite legally and above board – and take her away with me in my trailer."

Krista wanted to block her ears. How could this woman talk about Sugar as her "property"? Sugar wasn't an object – she was a living, breathing creature. And, as they'd seen out in the stable yard, she was obviously scared to death at the very sight of Julie Charlton.

"Would you mind if I try to contact Lee about this?" Jo asked, trying to remain calm. "After all, he handed over money for the pony in good faith."

Secret Whispers

"I don't see why you have to," Mrs Charlton objected. "I've explained the situation already."

But Jo insisted on calling Lee's number. She waited then shook her head. "Not available," she reported, clicking off the phone. "I have to admit, Lee never produced any papers as proof of ownership," she muttered.

"That's because Ian didn't have them – I did!"

"And I guess Lee wouldn't be too bothered about the formalities." Carefully Jo thought her way through the problem. "But if you still own the pony, and if you don't have anywhere other than your ex-husband's smallholding to stable her, which I presume you don't …"

"That's right!" Krista cried. "Where is Sugar going to live?"

My Magical Pony

Julie Charlton gave a loud tut. "Do you think I'm mad? I don't plan to keep the little nuisance!"

"What then?" Krista demanded. Suddenly she felt sick with worry over the pony's future.

"I'm going to sell her," Mrs Charlton informed them. "I'm going to take her to auction and not hold on to her a moment longer than is necessary!"

"What can I do?" Jo spread her hands in despair as she and Krista stood in the yard watching Julie Charlton attempting to force Sugar out of her stable into the nearby trailer. "I can't get in touch with Lee."

Secret Whispers

"Poor Sugar!" Krista put her hand over her eyes to block out the sight of Julie Charlton dragging the pony from the stable.

Mrs Charlton smacked the pony on the rump with a heavy, knotted rope, making her

shoot forward then rear up, only to be
dragged down again by a second rope
attached to her head collar.

Sugar neighed and squealed, thrashing
about on the end of the lead-rope.

"All your good work is going to waste,
Krista!" Jo sighed. "The poor little thing will
be back to square one after this."

Krista couldn't bear it. She ran forward to
stop Mrs Charlton.

"Stand clear!" Julie Charlton yelled as
Sugar reared up. "Do you want to get yourself
killed?"

"You'll never get her in the trailer like that!"
Krista cried. "She's scared of you. Stop yanking
at the rope!"

My Magical Pony

"Says the expert!" Julie Charlton scoffed. She raised the knotted rope, ready to strike again.

Krista couldn't let it happen. Quickly she grabbed Mrs Charlton's raised arm and pushed her backwards with all her might.

The woman overbalanced and lost hold of the rope. Sugar felt it slacken, reared yet again then galloped for the open gate.

But the parked trailer was in the way, and in her panic, Sugar swerved, changed direction and gave her cruel owner time to run and slam the gate.

"Come on, help me trap her in that corner by the tack room!" Mrs Charlton yelled at Jo and Krista.

My Magical Pony

Jo glanced at Krista, who shook her head. "What choice do we have?" Jo muttered, advancing with her arms raised wide, shooing the panicking pony towards the corner. "Come on, Krista, you know her better than anyone. And Sugar's going to injure herself if she keeps on throwing herself about!"

Krista knew this was true. A frightened horse would do anything – literally risk its own life – to escape danger. But helping to capture Sugar felt like the worst thing she'd ever had to do.

"There!" she murmured, trying to get close. "Calm down, girl!"

Sugar flicked an ear towards Krista, recognised her voice and hesitated. It gave

Secret Whispers

Julie Charlton time to sneak up on the far side.

"It's me – Krista!" she soothed, hating the sound of her own voice. "Stand still. Don't be scared."

Sugar looked at Krista with a big question mark in her eyes. *Do I still trust you?* she seemed to ask.

And this gave Mrs Charlton the chance to creep closer and slide a rope around the pony's neck, and time for Jo to herd her towards the trailer – "Gee-up!

My Magical Pony

Go on, get in!" – so that before Sugar knew what was happening, she was on the ramp and being rushed inside. Then the ramp was up and the door was bolted in place.

"Serves you right, you little nuisance!" Julie Charlton muttered as the trapped pony kicked and squealed. "The sooner I'm rid of you, the better!"

And Jo had to hold Krista back as Sugar's owner got into her car. "I'm disappointed in Lee," she confessed. "He should've checked out the papers when he bought her."

But Krista wasn't listening. She was breaking free and running after the trailer, trying to get one last look at Sugar inside the trailer as Mrs Charlton drove off down the lane.

Chapter Eight

Sugar, I'm so sorry! Krista said to herself. *You trusted me and I let you down!*

"Try not to feel too bad," Jo told her as the trailer disappeared. The silence hung heavy in the air. "There was nothing either of us could do."

But Krista wasn't ready to give in. She still had one thing left to try. "Do you mind if I don't stick around for the afternoon rides?" she asked as casually as she could.

Jo shook her head. "No, I understand. You need a break."

My Magical Pony

So Krista grabbed her jacket and set off in the direction of home. She didn't look back at Hartfell as she climbed the stile and began to jog along the cliff path. "Shining Star, I need you!" she said out loud. "I hope you can hear me!"

She ran over the rough ground until she came at last to the magic spot. She stopped and caught her breath. Above her head, white gulls soared in the bright blue sky.

"I need you to fly here as soon as you can," she told her magical pony. "I have to help Sugar, and I can't do it without you!"

Would Shining Star hear her? Would he be able to come?

Krista stared up into the sky. Then she lowered her gaze to the flat, glittering

horizon. She saw a tiny white boat sail slowly out to sea, but there was no silvery cloud drifting towards her, no magical pony beating his wings and scattering his dazzling dust.

So Krista turned towards the moor, still white with frost where the sun hadn't shone. She made out the jagged rocks at the top of the hill, and just one or two light clouds drifting low towards her. Her heart beat faster. Surely one of the clouds would melt away to reveal her beautiful magical pony.

"A woman came and snatched Sugar away from Hartfell," she murmured. "We have to save her and bring her back."

Slowly one cloud separated from the others. It grew bigger and brighter.

107

My Magical Pony

"Oh, thank you!" Krista sighed. Silver dust fell from the sky as the cloud broke and Shining Star appeared.

The magical pony gazed down on Krista. He hovered above the magic spot. "Tell me everything that has happened," he said slowly. "What has gone wrong since we last spoke?"

Star's strong presence calmed Krista. "There's been a fight over who owns Sugar," she reported. "A horrible woman called

Secret Whispers

Julie Charlton took her away."

"In what way was she horrible?" Star asked.

"She was cruel to Sugar. She hit her with a heavy rope."

This was enough for Shining Star to realise that they must rescue the Arab pony. "Where is Julie Charlton now?" he asked.

"I don't know. She went off in a car and I couldn't follow. That's why I came to find you."

"And what does she plan to do with Sugar?"

"She wants to take her to an auction and sell her. But Sugar will be scared stiff and she'll act up. No one will want to buy her."

"And then?" Star asked as Krista faltered.

"Then she'll be sold cheap to … well, to someone else who doesn't care about her."

My Magical Pony

She'd heard stories about unwanted ponies being bunched together and taken off in wagons to places she couldn't even bear to think about.

"More cruelty and neglect," Shining Star sighed. "Come, Krista, climb on my back. We must save Sugar before it's too late."

Krista sat astride Shining Star and held tight to his mane as they rose from the cliff path.

She looked down on the frozen moor and the wide expanse of glittering sea. "Maybe if we swoop down the hillside we'll be able to spot Mrs Charlton's car and trailer," she suggested.

So her magical pony beat his wide wings and flew low over the moor. Krista saw rooftops

nestled on the hillside. She recognised Hartfell, with its stables and paddocks, then picked out the lane that Julie Charlton had driven along.

"Slow down," she murmured, pointing out the road to Shining Star.

He flew slowly, scattering silver dust with every beat of his wings. They saw a farmer driving his tractor across a field, three walkers climbing a stile, a delivery van stopping at a farmhouse. But there was no sign of Julie Charlton's car and shabby silver trailer.

"It's too late, we've lost her," Krista muttered. They had reached the outskirts of Whitton and had to choose which direction to take.

111

Secret Whispers

"Where are we now?" Star asked, arching his neck and listening intently.

Krista leaned sideways and looked carefully at the scattering of houses nearby. "We're near Ian Charlton's place," she decided. "Look, that's his smallholding, down there!"

The magical pony nodded. "We will find answers to some of our questions here," he decided. "We must stop and take a look."

"But what about Mrs Charlton?" Krista argued. "She's got Sugar. We can't let her get away!"

"There are answers here," Star insisted. He flew lower still, over the house with its untidy outbuildings, then landed in a field close by.

And so Krista had to trust Shining Star's judgement, sliding from his back as he folded

113

his wings. She landed with a crunch on the frozen grass. "What now?"

"Go quietly and search the stables," Star urged. "Though the pony is not here now, there will be other clues. Find out as much as you can."

"And you'll wait here?" she checked.

He nodded. "Go. The afternoon is drawing to a close. Do not delay."

So Krista ran across the field towards Ian Charlton's place, careful to stay out of sight of the main house and heading straight for the outbuilding where Sugar had been stabled. She was climbing a wall into the rough yard when the house door opened and she had to duck behind a rusty tractor.

Secret Whispers

"OK, Ian, I'll take this old farm machinery off your hands," a voice said.

Krista peered round the side of the tractor wheel to see a man shaking hands with someone who must be Ian Charlton.

There was a muttered reply from inside the doorway then the first man nodded and walked towards his car. He started the engine and drove off.

Behind the tractor, Krista took a deep breath. She waited for the front door to close and for silence to fall. Then she crept on towards the stable.

Star says I need clues! she thought, pushing the old door on its rusty hinges. *But what kind? I don't even know what I'm looking for!*

My Magical Pony

In the gloom she saw the empty hay net hanging from the wall and the old barrow in one corner.

Krista was about to step inside when a loud voice stopped her.

"Hey, you!" Ian Charlton came striding from the house – a short man with dark, floppy hair that fell across his face. "This is private property. What do you think you're doing?"

Krista jumped back. She had to think of an excuse, and quick. "I came to see the pony!"

"It's not here any more," Charlton snapped, stepping across Krista's path.

She frowned back. "But I saw her here at New Year. I just thought …"

"I don't care what you were thinking!"

116

Secret Whispers

Krista backed off. But she refused to leave just yet. "I thought Mrs Charlton might have brought her back here," she said boldly.

Ian Charlton narrowed his eyes. "Mrs Charlton? What's she got to do with it?"

Krista had guessed rightly that Mr Charlton wasn't up to date with the latest development. "She came to Hartfell and took the pony. She said she owned her and had papers to prove it."

To Krista's surprise, Ian Charlton laughed out loud. "She's got a cheek!" he scoffed. "I knew Julie was after everything she could lay her hands on during the divorce, but I didn't think even she would stoop so low!"

Shocked, Krista waited in silence for Mr Charlton to calm down.

117

My Magical Pony

"Diamond Charm does not belong to my ex-wife," he insisted. "I owned her. I bought her two years ago and I'll show you the bill of sale to prove it."

"But what about the papers in the envelope?" Krista protested as she followed Mr Charlton into the kitchen. "Mrs Charlton said they proved that she owned the pony!"

"Did you actually read them?" he demanded, sifting through jumbled papers in a drawer and pulling out the one he wanted. "Bill of sale, made out to me!" he crowed. "It shows I had every right to sell Diamond Charm to Lee Harris."

Krista gasped and shook her head. "So Mrs Charlton played a trick on us?"

Secret Whispers

Ian Charlton nodded. "That's Julie for you. She'll make money out of me, whether it's legal or not. And you can tell Lee Harris he'd better get a move on if he wants his pony back."

Krista's head was in a whirl. She wanted to return to Shining Star and explain everything to him. "How come?" she asked.

"Because Netherby Horse Auction happens the first Friday of every month," Ian Charlton told her. "That's tomorrow. And you can bet your life that Julie will take the pony and sell her on faster than you can say 'Diamond Charm'!"

Chapter Nine

"Hurry, Shining Star! We have to get to Netherby!" Krista ran back to her magical pony with the urgent message.

He stood in the frosty field overlooking Whitton Sands. A cold wind blew his long mane clear of his beautiful, serious face. "What did you discover?"

"There's a big argument between the Charltons over who owned Sugar," she reported. "I've no idea who's right, but I do know that it's Netherby Auction tomorrow morning and that's where

Secret Whispers

Mrs Charlton is heading right now."

Star nodded. "Good. So now the race is on in earnest to save the little Arab. Come, Krista, climb up."

Quickly she scrambled on to Shining Star's back. "Netherby is about fifteen miles inland," she explained. "I reckon Julie Charlton has had time to get there and find somewhere to park overnight. She'll want to get Sugar to auction early tomorrow."

Smoothly Shining Star spread his wings and rose from the ground. Krista looked down at the Charltons' smallholding. "I hope I never have to come here again!" she muttered. "Horrible place, horrible people!"

Star flew silently on. In the west the sun

set with a red-gold glow over the sea. The earth below grew dark.

"Follow the river," Krista suggested, pointing out a route up a wide estuary to where the banks narrowed.

Her magical pony's white coat glittered, his gorgeous wings beat smoothly as he followed the course of the river inland. They flew over dark woods, over small villages and lonely houses, across fields bordering the river banks, until they came to a town.

"This is it!" Krista whispered. She recognised the old market square with its stone cross and a low, white pub overlooking the square. "But where does the auction take place?"

122

Secret Whispers

"Not here in the centre of town," Shining Star guessed. "Is there somewhere with wide open spaces, where people can drive their trailers and wagons?"

Krista thought hard. "Let's try the show-ground," she decided. "That's where they do the show-jumping and farmers enter their sheep and cattle into competitions. It's on the far side of the river."

So, as orange streetlights glimmered and came on, Shining Star flew silently over the town. On the outskirts he found the wide gates of the show-ground and together they read a big notice nailed to a post.

"Stop here!" Krista muttered. She didn't care if she had to wait all night in the freezing cold,

just so long as she could stop Julie Charlton from selling Sugar.

"I do not like this place," Shining Star murmured uneasily. "I hear the cries of many creatures. I smell fear."

Stepping to the ground in the middle of a big arena, Krista shivered as she looked around. She pictured unwilling horses being led into the ring, crowds pressing against the barriers for a closer look, buyers coolly calculating how much each animal was worth. "Let's walk around," she suggested.

Secret Whispers

Shining Star led the way from the arena towards a large gravelled area to one side. In the last glimmer of daylight, Krista read a list of parking charges on a nearby notice and then spotted half a dozen horse-boxes already parked up for the night on the far side of the car park. She drew a sharp breath. "I bet one of those belongs to Julie Charlton!"

"Perhaps ..." Star whispered. "But we do not want her to see us. We must go quietly and carefully."

Realising that he was right, Krista held back. She pointed out a clump of trees beyond the parked trailers. "Let's go down the bank and stay out of sight by the river until we get to those trees. We can creep into

125

the shadows and take a good look from there
without being seen!"

Shining Star nodded and let Krista lead
the way. She soon found an overgrown
footpath and they made good progress. A few
minutes later, they were level with the trees
and making their way up the river bank again.

But by now it was really dark and Krista
stumbled over a thick root as she crept
through the wood. She fell to her knees.
Shining Star lowered his head. "Did you hurt
yourself?" he asked.

Krista shook her head. They were very
close to the parked vehicles, the nearest of
which was a horse-box large enough to
transport four or five horses. Next to it was a

126

Secret Whispers

smart trailer for two. Krista held her breath and looked down the silent row. At the very end she saw something that made her gasp.

"Is that what we are looking for?" Star whispered.

Krista nodded as she made sure that this was Julie Charlton's car and trailer. "It looks empty," she muttered, creeping closer. "What has she done with Sugar?"

"Wait," Star warned. He listened carefully. "The pony is in the trailer. She stands without moving, scarcely breathing for fear. But she is there."

"And there's no sign of Mrs Charlton!" Krista whispered. "Trust her to leave poor Sugar locked up in a dark trailer all alone!"

My Magical Pony

The thought of the little Arab standing paralysed with fear not ten paces from where they were hiding was too much for Krista. "I'm going to let her out!" she insisted, creeping clear of the trees and climbing a low fence. Before

Shining Star could stop her, she had run round to the back of the trailer and peered inside.

The sudden movement made Sugar kick out.

Secret Whispers

Her back hooves clattered against the metal side of the trailer. In the horse-box next door, other horses shifted uneasily.

"Don't be scared!" Krista pleaded. All she could make out was Sugar's dark shape and the dim white star on her forehead. "It's me, Krista!"

There was no time to lose. The nearby horses were stamping their feet and whinnying, and surely someone would soon come to find out what was causing the racket. As Krista talked and tried to soothe Sugar, she slid the bolts and let down the ramp. "Take it easy, little girl," she murmured softly. "You know me, I'm here to help."

From inside the trailer Sugar saw the

dark, open space of the car park. She saw Krista standing at the top of the ramp, and in the distance, running across the empty space towards them, she spotted the figure of a woman.

"Leave that pony alone!" Julie Charlton cried. She'd been sitting in the show-ground café, drinking coffee with a friend, when the two women had heard a disturbance in the car park. Alarm bells had rung inside Julie's head and she'd run out to see what was going on. She was on the scene just in time to see the kid from Hartfell lowering the ramp and setting the pony loose.

Shocked and confused, Krista froze to the spot.

130

Secret Whispers

Meanwhile, Sugar had only one thought in her head – escape!

She reared up with a fiery look, rolling her eyes and flattening her ears.

The angry woman was growing closer. She would come and slam the door shut, the iron bolts would slide back into place …

Sugar landed on all fours and charged. She brushed Krista to one side, sending her tumbling off the ramp. *Freedom!*

She was out in the open, the dark night beckoned.

Julie Charlton flung up her arms trying to stop the fleeing pony.

But Sugar galloped on.

Chapter Ten

"See what you've done!" Julie Charlton was furious with Krista. "Tell me what we do now – go on, tell me, you idiot!"

Krista's heart beat fast as she got up from the ground. There was chaos in the car park. More people came running from the café and a car sped through the gates. Sugar galloped down the river bank, out of sight.

The car skidded to a halt and Ian Charlton jumped out. "This is your fault!" he stormed at his ex-wife, quickly taking in the scene that greeted him. "I know what you're up to,

and you'd no right to bring that pony here in the first place!"

"Well, it doesn't matter now, because this kid has gone and let her loose!" Mrs Charlton cried. "She's galloped off, who knows where!"

"And it serves you right!" Mr Charlton yelled.

"Yeah, yeah. Whatever!"

As the two angry grown-ups launched into a full-scale row, Krista seized her chance to slip away. She ran back to the deep shadow of the trees, her heart pounding, her mouth dry.

"Come!" Shining Star said. "We will follow the pony."

Within seconds Krista was on her magical pony's back and they flew from under the trees towards the river bank where they had last seen

Sugar. "I couldn't stop her from running away," Krista gasped. "It all happened too fast."

"You meant well and it is done now," Star said. He searched the steep riverbanks for signs of the fleeing pony, heading back the way they had come.

"It's hopeless," Krista muttered, seeing only blackness and the dull glint of the river running towards the sea.

But Shining Star searched on. "The pony will flee until she can flee no more. Then she must stop."

Already Krista caught the salty smell of the sea in the night air. The river broadened and the lights of Whitton beckoned.

It was then that Star caught sight of the

Secret Whispers

runaway, stumbling up the bank and cutting across the moor to avoid the town lights ahead. "She is tired," he told Krista. "Her legs will go no further."

Krista gripped Star's mane and looked down at the dark stretch of moor. She could see Sugar struggling up the hillside – a lonely, frightened pony who could scarcely run another step. "Will she let us help her?" Krista wondered.

My Magical Pony

Her magical pony flew ahead of Sugar and landed. As he folded his wings, a silver glow spread across the moor.

Exhausted, Sugar stopped at a safe distance from Shining Star and Krista.

"What now?" Krista asked. "If I make a wrong move, Sugar will run off again."

"Remember, Krista, you know this pony. You are her friend."

Krista nodded. Now was the time to concentrate hard and use the skills that Lee had had taught her. First of all, she had to read Sugar's signals – head up, ears back, breathing hard. "She's still scared," she told Star. "She's looking straight at us, warning us not to go near."

Secret Whispers

"Good," Shining Star murmured. "We must wait."

Be patient! Krista told herself. *Read the signs.* She stood perfectly still as Sugar swished her tail. "Good girl," she whispered. "Take your time."

Sugar's heart beat hard against her ribs. She didn't want to run, yet she was still afraid.

"Don't worry, you're safe," Krista murmured. "You don't want to be alone in the dark. You want to be with us."

The pony heard the gentle voice and saw that Krista meant her no harm. Slowly, bit by bit, she lowered her head towards the ground.

Wonderful! Krista picked up the longed-for moment when Sugar invited her in. She stepped towards her.

My Magical Pony

I know this girl. She is good to me. Sugar stood
still as Krista approached.

Slowly Krista raised her hand and stroked
Sugar. Smoothly she put her arm around the
pony's neck.

The lights were on at Hartfell as Krista walked
with Shining Star and Sugar up the hill. Star
decided to wait under a hawthorn tree in the
lane; the magical pony was Krista's secret,
never to be shared with anyone.

"Wait for me?" Krista whispered.

He nodded.

"Easy, girl," Krista said softly to the Arab
pony, who hesitated. "You're doing well. You're
going to be fine."

138

Secret Whispers

In the yard at Hartfell, Lee and Jo waited to greet them.

"Don't be scared," Krista told Sugar. "Lee won't let anything bad happen to you."

Sure enough, the tall New Zealander came to the gate. "Hey, Krista, that must have been one impressive piece of horse communication!" he grinned. "The last we heard from Ian Charlton was that Sugar had cut loose and run."

He closed the gate as Krista and Sugar walked into the yard. "Ian called to give me the latest news about the pony auction

and the fight he'd had there with his ex.
Pretty ugly, huh?"

Krista nodded. "We – I – finally caught up
with Sugar just outside Whitton. So what
happened in the end between the Charltons?"

"Mrs C finally admitted that she'd made up
the stuff about the pony's papers. I've got the
real ones here." He patted the back pocket of
his jeans. "It's just a pity I wasn't here when
she first showed up."

"Yeah, where were you?" Krista grumbled,
smiling at Jo and walking Sugar into her
comfy stable.

From next-door Shandy gave Sugar a
welcoming whinny.

"I had to go fix a friend's horse. He'd

140

Secret Whispers

entered him into a New Year steeplechase.
The stable lad was heavy-handed and ended
up turning the horse box-shy. He needed a
little work, that's all."

"And will we have to start over again with
Sugar?" Krista asked, moving quietly around
the stable, settling the pony into a deep bed
of straw. "She had a really bad time while you
were away."

"Hey," Lee pointed out, "Jo tells me you
already had a saddle on her."

"But that was before …"

"And look what you just did to find her
and bring her back here all by yourself!"

"It wasn't just me …" Krista began then
stopped suddenly.

Lee glanced quickly across the yard. "So who else was there to help?"

"Nobody!" Krista blushed. Now that Sugar was safe, she was eager to dash back to Shining Star.

"So tomorrow we carry on with Sugar where you left off," Lee said, full of quiet confidence. He smiled as his pony came up and nuzzled his shoulder.

"And you'll teach me more secrets." Krista smiled happily then backed out of the stable.

"Where are you dashing off to now?" Jo asked.

Secret Whispers

"Nowhere! Won't be long!" Krista was across
the yard and running down the lane, just in
time to see Shining Star rise from the ground.

"Well?" he asked her, gently beating his
wings.

She looked up and felt his warm glow on
her face. "Good!" she told him. "Everything
worked out fine!"

My Magical Pony

The magical pony had one last piece of advice. "Look after Sugar, Krista. Show her the love that her life has lacked so far."

"I – we – will!" she promised. She and Lee would work together. Soon the hardships of Sugar's past life would be a distant memory.

Satisfied, Shining Star rose higher. "Goodbye, Krista," he said, scattering his silver dust.

She felt it fall all around. "Thank you," she whispered.

She watched Star fly away then turned and carried the biggest secret of all back with her to Hartfell. The secret of her magical pony.